anythink

Daphne, Secret Vlogger

Daphne, Secret Vlogger is published by Stone Arch Books
A Capstone Imprint
1710 Roe Crest Drive
North Mankato, Minnesota 56003
www.mycapstone.com

Library of Congress Cataloging-in-Publication Data is available on the
Library of Congress website.

Summary: Annabelle Louis is a new kid and a nobody at McManus
Middle School. Her therapist challenges the ever-skeptical Annabelle to
try new things and make new friends to help her cope with her mom's
upcoming military assignment in Afghanistan. Annabelle takes the
opportunity to create a secret online vlog, *Daphne Doesn't*, where she
makes fun of all the things she thinks are a waste of time, and agrees to
give sports a try . . . reluctantly. Undercover as Daphne, Annabelle makes
fun of sports like lacrosse (Why does everyone look like they're chasing
butterflies?) and swimming (Poodle hair and wedgies? No thanks!).
But when kids around school start viewing and sharing *Daphne Doesn't*,
Annabelle's troubles are just beginning!

ISBN 978-1-4965-6294-4 (library-bound hardcover)
ISBN 978-1-4965-6298-2 (paperback)
ISBN 978-1-4965-6302-6 (eBook PDF)

Cover illustration by Marcos Calo
Design by Kay Fraser

Printed and bound in Canada.
PA020

DAPHNE
Definitely
DOESN'T DO
SPORTS

by Tami Charles

STONE ARCH BOOKS
a capstone imprint

Definitely doesn't do sports Definitely doesn't do drama Definitely doesn't do fashion Definitely doesn't do dances Definitely doesn't do Definitely doesn't do sports Definitely doesn't do drama Definitely doesn't do fashion Definitely doesn't do dances Definitely doesn't do sports Definitely doesn't do drama Definitely doesn't do fashion Definitely doesn't do dances Definitely doesn't do sports Definitely doesn't do drama Definitely doesn't do Sports

1

ALWAYS ON THE MOVE!

Confession #1: My life is one big movie series.

Confession #2: Some of the movies are "in my head." Some are as real as the ones on my MacBook computer.

Here's the latest horror film that took place yesterday in the Louis household.

Disclaimer: Some scenes may (or may not) be exaggerated for dramatic effect.

The opening credits roll in, slow and bold. . . .

Always on the Move:
The Sad, Lonely Life of an Air Force Brat
Starring: Annabelle Daphne Louis
Directed by: Annabelle Daphne Louis

It all begins on a dark and stormy Friday evening. Dad makes dinner—a fall-off-the-bone Puerto Rican stewed chicken dish called *pollo guisado*. If you have never eaten this, then you don't know what it means to feel alive.

"Family meeting in the living room!" Mom announces, just as I'm sopping up the last forkful.

We all take a seat on the carpet, because we're not completely moved in to the new house yet. Outside, the wind is smacking a tree branch against the window. Gotta love when nature adds its own special effects. Mom lights a few candles and clicks the dimmer on the light remote. Dad clears his throat and lets out one long-winded breath. If I didn't know any better, I would think they were about to summon a ghost.

And cue camera zoom . . .

Mom starts talking. "Annabelle, we wanted to tell you the real reason we've moved to Linden. . . ."

The camera is zoomed in so close to my face, I'm sure the audience can see every freckle. The skin under my eyes sinks lower and lower as seconds turn to minutes and Mom draws out her speech. The audio fades in and out, and all I hear are words like "leave" and "assignment" and "alone."

The words mix together. I try to shake the scene out of my head and get back to focus. But then it hits me.

"What did you say, Mom? You're getting . . . what?" My throat tightens.

TDY . . . TDY . . . TDY . . .

Temporary duty yonder. Fancy Air Force words for Mom's leaving—this time without us. "Wait, there's more," Mom says.

Ladies and gentlemen, we have a sequel.

Dad adds in his piece. "Since this will be

Mom's last assignment before retiring next year, we're going to stay in Linden and live civilian life. She'll commute to Fort Dix for work until it's time for her TDY. And with the transfer, I landed a new Cisco client based in New York, which means I have to travel into the city a few times a week, so—"

"Wait. Slow down," I say. "What about homeschooling, Dad?"

Mom and Dad lock hands and look at each other, then back at me. I know what's coming.

I am going to middle school. Real school, with teachers and seventh graders and eyeballs and *gym.*

"You guys tricked me!" I'm standing now. The camera angles upward to make me appear larger than I am.

Just a week ago, we were living happily ever after in Germany, where Mom was Master Sergeant in the Air Force and Dad worked from home for Cisco, all while homeschooling me. Life was perfectly fine. Then Mom comes home one day and announces we're headed to the city she once lived in—Linden, New Jersey, land of Targets, Starbucks, and an oil refinery that occasionally makes the whole city smell like a gigantic fart. Her words, not mine.

She's been acting funny ever since. Extra clingy with me. Extra lovey-dovey kissy-face with Dad. UGH!

Mom and Dad spring to their feet too. The camera pans up and then zooms out.

The next scene plays out like a game of verbal Ping-Pong, with me asking questions and Mom firing back answers.

ME

How long will you be gone?

MOM

Six months, not much longer.

(A ghost whizzes by and punches ME right in the throat.)

ME

Why can't Dad and I go with you, like we
always do?

MOM

I'm sorry, Annabelle. This is not like it was before in the UK, Spain, and Germany. I cannot bring you to Afghanistan. You understand, *schätzchen*?

(MOM calls ME "sweetie" in German to soften the blow. It usually works. Not this time.)

ME

When do you leave?

MOM

After Christmas.

(Insert massive thought bubble above my head. That's four months from now. DAD grabs ME by the shoulders and pulls ME in for a hug. I transform into ice, blocking out his warmth.)

ME

It's bad enough you guys moved me away from the one friend I have. Now you expect me to start all over again?

(My eyes are stinging now. I will not cry. I will not cry.)

DAD

This will be a big change for everyone, Annabelle, but together we'll get through it.

(DAD refuses to let ME go. Zoom in on MOM, wrapping her arms around us. The warmth of MOM and DAD melts my ice block, even though I don't want it to. Outside, the rain stops falling. The tree branch no longer smacks against the window. And that imaginary ghost has faded into oblivion.)

MOM

Everything will be fine, Annabelle. My Air Force buddy, Pete Fingerlin, is the counselor at McManus Middle School. He set you up with a buddy to give you a tour bright and early Monday morning.

ME *(thinking)*

Buddy? Sounds like a code word for babysitter. Call me psychic, but I have a feeling this whole middle school thing will go horribly wrong.

End scene!

2

TEXTING ACROSS THE POND

Mae: Belle! How's life in the US? Missing you here in the UK. :'(

Me: New country. New house. New school. New problems. Over it.

Mae: SCHOOL? Like with other humans?

Me: Apparently Mom and Dad forgot that I'm allergic to formal education.

Mae: That's awful! When do you start?

Me: T minus 4 hrs., 38 mins. Run away with me?

Mae: Oy! I forgot about the time difference. Get some sleep!

Me: About to start a new novel with Dad. *Enchanted Air.* Margarita Engle strikes again! Missing our father-daughter homeschooling sessions . . .

Mae: You'll survive . . . maybe. ;) FaceTime ya before you leave. Sweet dreams!

3

LINDEN HATES ME

The FaceTime ringer beeps just as I'm getting ready for jail. I mean, school. Mae Tanaka—best friend, keeper of promises. "I still can't believe your parents sprung all of this on you!" Mae says as soon as I open my iPad.

When Mom was stationed in the UK, Mae and I were among the rare kids who preferred to be homeschooled rather than go to a new school every other year. That's the life of an Air Force kid. Too many moves.

Too many desperate attempts to make new friends.

Because both of our dads were techies who worked from home, Mae and I had the perfect setup. Our dads would take turns teaching us. My dad would take the morning shift to teach us math, technology, and sciences. And in the afternoon, Mr. Tanaka taught us how to use "nature as our classroom." We'd paint in the park, take strolls around the lake, and study foreign languages. Ah, those were the good old days.

There's a knock at my door, and I already know who it is.

"Hold on. Mom alert." I crack the door open.

Mom weasels her face inside and looks at me, frowning because I'm still in my robe. "Need help getting dressed?" she asks, still wearing her *I'm-sorry* face.

"No, Mom. I'm fine. Plus, I'm FaceTiming with Mae for a couple minutes."

"Tell her hello, and don't take too long.

I wouldn't want you to be late to your meeting."

Honestly, I've had enough meetings for one lifetime.

I hurry back to my iPad. It's almost seven o'clock. That doesn't give me much time, so I speed my way through everything that's happened over the weekend. Mom's TDY. The new school. The ridiculous school tour with a "buddy."

I end my rant with, "So basically my life is ruined."

Mae hits me with, "No, it isn't. You'll be amazing, Annabelle!"

Typical Mae. All rainbows and sunshine and bubbles.

I prop the iPad on my dresser. "Hold on while I get dressed," I tell her.

"Ooh, what are you going to wear?" she asks. "I can't even picture doing algebra in anything besides my pajamas."

I have yet to receive all of my boxes from

Germany. In my closet there are three boxes I still haven't unpacked. "I haven't had time to even think about that," I say, growing more frustrated as I look for clothes. "You know," Mae says, "I heard Americans like color. Look for something that stands out. Ooh, like Lady Gaga!"

"I'd rather snack on broken glass."

"Just trust me!" Mae laughs.

At the bottom of one of the boxes, I find an oversized orange plaid shirt and purple leggings. I shuffle over to my dresser, still wrapped in my robe, and hold up the outfit.

"Gaga enough?" I ask.

"Oh, that's perfect!" Mae says. "Now you just need shoes."

In the closet, I find my favorite pair—teal Converse sneaker-boots. "I'm pretty sure I've forgotten how this social thing works, Mae," I say as I pull them on. "Like, who am I supposed to have lunch with? Aren't there rules and reserved tables?" I sigh, then I pop my face back on the screen.

"Ta-da!" I stand back so Mae can get a better view of my outfit.

At first she doesn't say anything, just gives a long stare.

"Oh, no. You think I look awful, don't you?" I ask.

"Actually, no." Mae's voice gets really soft. "I think you look perfect. I just miss you is all."

I hold two fingers to my heart and wait for her to do it back. That's our thing, the number two. Because even though miles and seas and time zones separate us, we're always going to be two *amigas*, the best two mates there ever were.

There's a rapid knock on my door.

"I have to go now, Mae."

"Send me a text and let me know how it goes."

I blow her a kiss and hang up. Before I can even open my door, Mom comes in, uninvited, and plops on my bed.

"I'm sorry, Annabelle," she apologizes for the trillionth time.

"I'll be OK, Mom," I lie, cold and quick.

"At least you have one thing to look forward to—having a separate girl cave." Mom smiles.

My girl cave has always been in the same room as my bedroom. But with this big house, my parents promised me a room in the basement. I want to be excited, but this school thing ruined it.

"Oh, come on, Annabelle. You have to be just a little excited for your first day!"

"But it's not the first day, Mom. School started weeks ago when we were still in Germany. You do know what this means, don't you?"

"I hope you're not worried about falling behind."

"It's not about the work," I say. "It's that by now everybody has formed their circles. That's how school works. That's why I stopped going in the first place. And now you guys are throwing me to the sharks!"

I look at myself in the mirror and contemplate doing something with my hair. In Germany the weather was kinder to my curls. Judging by the way my hair is poofing out, Linden already hates me.

Mom lifts off the bed and stands behind me in the mirror.

"You look great, *schätzchen*. You'll amaze everyone with your charm and wit. Those kids will be begging to be your friend. I just know it!"

I'm not so sure.

4

JUST THE NEW KID

Mom and Dad insist on not only driving me to school but also on going inside to see the counselor, Mr. Fingerlin, and my assigned "buddy."

Side note: *Is it just me, or does the name Fingerlin make you want to eat something greasy?*

We're all silent in the car. Dad turns on the radio, blasts the volume, and starts dancing. All of a sudden the rapper starts bragging about how much money he spent on clothing.

"Seventy-five hundred dollars on a coat? Man, I don't get this *new* kind of music!" Dad yells over the beat.

He and Mom start laughing. I can't help it, so I laugh too. And for the first time in a while, it feels like we're back to our old selves again, the laugh-till-we-snort Louis trio.

Dad pulls up in front of McManus, and the red entry doors seem a thousand miles away. He lowers the music, and I let out a heavy sigh.

"We'll do the tour with you, Annabelle. Help you ease in," Dad says.

"That would be super embarrassing. Please don't!"

Dad turns around to say something else, but Mom's already slamming the car door behind her and marching her heels straight up to the school.

I grab my knapsack and make a beeline toward her, stumbling over my untied Converse sneaker-boot. I could have sworn I tied it back at home. I catch myself before falling, quickly tie it again, and keep it moving.

Mr. Fingerlin and my "buddy" are opening the doors by the time I reach Mom. I'm out of breath, Dad is shuffling behind me, and Mom is giving Mr. Fingerlin a bear hug. They're slapping each other's backs so hard I can hear their ribs vibrate.

"Aim high!" Mr. Fingerlin throws his bald head back and points his face to the sky.

Then, on cue, Mom says, "Fly, fight, win!"

Dad shakes Mr. Fingerlin's hand and that turns into another hug.

"It's been a long time, Ruben. Good to see you!" Mr. Fingerlin says.

Buddy and I just stand there, staring at each other. She's legs-up-to-her-neck, supermodel tall. The sun is beaming down on her, creating a halo around her dark brown braids, matchy-matchy outfit, and sparkly red nail polish.

"This is Annabelle."

I don't look up when Dad says this. I just

zoom in on my Converse sneaker-boot, which is untied again. A clear sign that even my shoes want to break free of this place!

"Pleasure to meet you." Mr. Fingerlin shakes my hand firmly. "Wendy and I go way back to our Academy days in Colorado. She was always tougher and smarter than me. And look at her now. Master Sergeant!"

"Thank you for agreeing to meet with us so early, Pete," Mom says.

"No problem. Forgive me. This is Rachael Myers." Mr. Fingerlin points to Buddy girl. She gives a weak smile and shakes all of our hands.

"Look at that! You already have a friend, and the day is just beginning!" Mom's voice is beyond excited.

Great. A forced friendship is just what I need.

"Rachael will show you around before the day starts," Mr. Fingerlin says.

"Mom, Dad, I have it from here. You can leave now. OK?" I say with my teeth pressed together.

"You sure, *schätzchen*?"

"Bless you!" Rachael says to Mom.

"Oh!" Mom chuckles. "I didn't sneeze, dear. I was calling Annabelle my little—"

"Mom!" I cough one time. "I'll see you when I get home."

"Can't wait to hear all about your first day. *Viel glück!*" Mom winks at me.

Rachael's eyebrows rise half an inch.

The back of my neck is burning as they head toward the exit. Dad walks like a normal human, and of course Mom is walking backward, blowing kisses at me before she disappears out the door.

"Let's get started!" Mr. Fingerlin hands me a folder with my schedule and papers of all the activities McManus has to offer. He explains that Rachael is the president of the Positive Behavior in Schools (PBIS) club and they do character-building activities for the school community. The more he talks, the more I start to think that PBIS stands for *Practically Babysitting Incoming Students*. I want no part, and, judging by Rachael's lack of enthusiasm, neither does she.

"And now, I'll have Rachael take over. I'll be in my office if you ladies need me." Mr. Fingerlin walks down the hall in the opposite direction.

Rachael starts walking, and I follow.

"Yo," she says, "what in the world did your mom say to you before she left?"

"She wished me good luck."

"You from Russia or something?"

"Germany. But I was born here."

Rachael stops short and whips around. One of her long braids smacks me right in the nose. "They got black people in Germany?"

I knew that was coming. Off base in Germany, sometimes I felt like people stared at me like I was a circus act. I see it's not going to be any different here.

"Well, yeah," I say. "Not a lot of black people, though. Mom's in the Air Force, so we move a lot."

Rachael makes a face that I can't quite read.

Then she grabs my folder and takes a look at my schedule. "All right, I'll make this quick. Hope you're a fast learner." Rachael zips around the whole school in what feels like five minutes, every word coming out faster like she wants to hurry up and get this over with. Cafeteria. Gym. Auditorium—"for useless assemblies." My homeroom, 201, which is also Rachael's. And the locations of the rest of my classes. By the time we're back at the entrance of the school, I don't remember a thing.

Our last stop is the bathroom.

"The bell's gonna ring soon, so I have to put my face on."

I look at Rachael, puzzled. *But your face is on . . . right?* Of course, I don't say that, I just trail inside behind her.

She pulls a fuzzy, pink bag out of her backpack. The next part plays out like a Hollywood glamour short film. Off screen, a fan is blowing. Better yet, there are two people—one at each side—moving gigantic fans up and down. Rachael's braids whip against the wind. The camera zooms in as she starts to umm . . . *put her face on*. Lip gloss. Mascara. Black pencil on her eyelids.

The camera pans right, and the lenses have to refocus when they get to me because apparently my entire outfit is distorting the image. I don't know why, but I start looking at my reflection in the full-length mirror compared to hers: my purple leggings, which are sagging, thanks to the fact that my whole body is made up of parallel lines, compared to her form-fitting, curve-hugging blue jeans. My old, worn-out Converse, compared to her spotless Nike sneakers. My hair, which is playing a game of *Which curl can touch the ceiling first?* compared to hers, which apparently grows downward.

"Want some lip gloss?" Rachael jolts me out of the scene.

I swallow. "No, I'm fine. I left mine at home."

"You know, for a black German girl, you speak good English. Like no accent or anything."

The tension in my shoulders loosens a bit. A voice inside whispers, *Play it cool, Annabelle.*

"Well, English is my first language." I hop on the sink counter and lean against the wall. "We moved bases a lot and lived in Germany for a while, so I picked up on German. Dad's half Puerto Rican, so he taught me Spanish, and my best friend is Japanese, so she and her dad taught me a little of that too."

I'm almost ready to mention living in the UK. You know, hit her with the good stuff. But then I feel my left butt cheek turn wet, and I start to slide off the side of the sink counter.

"Whoa, you OK?" Rachael catches my wrist before I fall.

"Yeah . . . *totally.*" I pull my shirt down to hide the water stain on my butt.

"You're like a walking, breathing globe." Rachael laughs.

Then I start laughing too. And there we are,

laughing together like two *amigas*. Really, I'm not sure if Rachael meant that as a compliment or an insult, but who cares! If only Mom, Dad, and Mae could see me now!

The bell rings, and outside the halls get loud—fast. Rachael tosses her makeup in the pink bag and beelines it for the door. She turns quickly. "Good luck, umm . . . what was your name again?"

My heart plummets to the floor. "Annabelle."

I'm not sure if she hears me, because she's already opening the bathroom door. There's a crowd outside, and they're all waiting for *her*, like the paparazzi. They're taking selfies with Rachael and saying things like:

"You slaying that outfit, girl!"

"Great lip gloss shade, bae!"

"I'll cut off my pinky toe and donate it to science if you sit next to me in homeroom."

OK, the last one might be a stretch. But seriously, this exact scene is why I don't do school.

"Who's that?" one of her adoring fans asks.

Rachael stops selfie-posing for a split second and says, "Oh, that's just the new kid."

The bell rings, and just like that they all rush to homeroom. Without me.

5

THE DAY GETS BETTER

As I near homeroom, I hear noise and commotion. I take a deep breath and pray that no one notices me so I can quickly find a seat. Here goes nothing.

The chaos stops as soon as I get to the doorway. The whole class is staring at me. If this were a movie, the houselights would dim, and the spotlight would land right on my horrified face.

The teacher stops writing on the board and

turns to me. "You must be our new student! I'm Mrs. Rodriguez." She walks over and grabs my hand to shake it. "Well, don't just stand there. Come in! Come in!" Mrs. Rodriguez grabs me by the shoulders, walks me inside, and plants me dead smack in front of the room.

I have an audience. Lovely.

"Class, we have a new student!" she says.

I try my best not to look at anyone, though I see Rachael and company and I feel everyone's eyeballs glued to me.

"Go on. Introduce yourself, . . ."—Mrs. Rodriguez looks at her roster to double-check my name—"Annabelle."

My eyes find the floor. I whisper, "My name is Annabelle. Annabelle Louis."

"Speak up!" Jerk #1, for $500.

"We can't hear you." Jerk #2, double the money.

"Yo, is she a student or the janitor?" Jerk #3 wins it all!

The whispers spill out. I stay busy looking at the tile patterns on the floor.

"She's from Germany, y'all!" It's Rachael. At least she remembered that.

"Is that where she got those kicks from?" someone pipes up. "'Cause I ain't never seen nothing like those in the mall!"

The whole class erupts into talking and laughter.

That's it. I'm never coming back. I don't care if Dad is going back to work. I'll homeschool myself.

"OK, class, that's enough!" Mrs. Rodriguez screams, and that shuts them up. "You may find an empty seat, Annabelle."

I half look up at the desks aligned in perfect, mile-long rows, praying there's a seat right in the front so I can put an end to the museum exhibit that is Annabelle Louis. But nope, *nada*.

"There's one back here!" A smiling kid with a mouth full of braces stands up and beckons me to come join him.

"Ooooh!" someone calls out.

I can't take one more second, so I speed-walk to the back of the room where Brace Face is happily waiting for me. You'd think things couldn't get any worse, but my shoelace decides now is the proper time to find the floor. Again. By the time I realize it, it's too late. My right foot finds the left lace and . . .

TIMBERRRRR!

I go tumbling.

My knapsack goes airborne. Brace Face catches it before my pencils, notebooks, and MacBook fall out.

"SAFE!" he yells, holding it up like it's a trophy.

The class is laughing. I'm dying. Brace Face is smiling like he's the king of seventh grade. Mrs. Rodriguez is telling everyone to quiet down so she can take attendance.

I'm definitely going to YouTube some homeschooling videos as soon as I finish setting up my girl cave.

Everyone settles down after attendance. Then Mrs. Rodriguez starts to write some words on the board: SPORTS DAY!

A lot of the kids start cheering.

"Don't forget that Sports Day is next Wednesday. Who would like to stand up, introduce themselves, and tell Annabelle what that means?" Mrs. Rodriguez looks around the room hopefully.

Brace Face doesn't waste a second. He bolts out of his seat and squares his shoulders. "Hello, Annabelle. My name is Johnathan Lopez, but you can call me John. Welcome to McManus! Sports Day is cool because for one whole day, all of our academic classes are replaced by sports. We get to check out the different sports that McManus has to offer. Everybody gets a chance to play. That'll help you decide if you want to try out for a team. Personally, I've got my eyes on the swim team."

Two students clap—a girl and a boy seated in front of us.

John takes a bow and flashes me a shiny smile.

"Excellent! Thank you, Johnathan," Mrs. Rodriguez says. "I'm going to pass around a list of what you'll need to bring for each activity."

Mrs. Rodriguez walks around passing out our individual Sports Day assignments. "We had to place you where we could, since you joined us a little late," she says when she reaches me.

I take the paper and stuff it into my knapsack. Doesn't matter anyway because I won't be here by next Wednesday.

John leans toward me and asks, "What sports did you get?"

I don't even look at him as I shrug.

"Don't worry. The day gets better, Annabelle. Promise."

The bell rings. I toss my knapsack over my shoulder and get out of there as fast as I can.

6

TEXTING FROM BASE

Mom: *Schätzchen*! *Mi amor*! My love! I'm working a double shift, so can't talk on the phone. BUT TEXT ME ABOUT YOUR FIRST DAY! <3

Fifteen minutes later . . .

Mom: Annabelle, you there?

Mom to Group, Belle, Dad:

Ruben, please don't tell me you forgot

to pick up our daughter from school!

Dad to Group, Belle, Mom:

I picked her up . . . on time. She's locked away in her girl cave. She won't talk to me.

Mom to Group, Belle, Dad:

Annabelle, we'll talk about everything as soon as I get home. OK, sweetie?

Three hours later . . .

Belle to Group, Mom, Dad:

There's nothing to talk about. Effective immediately, I'm dropping out of middle school.

7

DAPHNE DOESN'T

Me and my big mouth! (Or should I say fingers.)

As soon as I clicked send, my parents sprang into action. Mom left work early, sped up the highway, and hit me with a lecture as soon as she got home: *There shall be no dropping out of anything, young lady. Not when I busted my butt getting three degrees! We don't do failure in this family!*

I've been carrying out my sentence at McManus Middle School ever since. And to make things a little more interesting, Mom thought it would be a good idea for me to see a therapist.

So here I am pacing the wooden floors in the doctor's office, puzzled by the googly-eyed horse heads protruding from the walls. There are four of them, half black, half brown hair sticking out in midair, staring me down like I'm hiding a carrot in my back pocket. And they don't look too happy right about now. That makes five of us.

Still in uniform, Mom is seated on a leather couch next to large double windows.

Dr. Varma walks in with a gigantic smile and caked-on makeup that's way too pale for her brown skin.

"Pleasure to meet you, Master Sergeant Louis. Thank you for your service."

Mom rises and shakes Dr. Varma's hand. "Pleasure's all mine."

"And this must be Annabelle?"

"Hi." I keep my eyes on her wedge sandals.

"Ah, she's shy, I see," Dr. Varma says,

like she's known me my whole life. *"Herzlich willkommen.* Welcome!"

"Danke!" I thank her, surprised to be feeling a little more relaxed now. "You speak German?"

"My dad served in Germany, like your mum. And in the UK and Japan too. We moved around quite a bit, just like you. I bet you know a few different languages."

Three years in Japan, two and a half years a piece in Spain and the UK, and five years in Germany will do that.

"Oh, I speak a bit of this and that," I say, shrugging.

Dr. Varma asks Mom to sit in the waiting room while we talk. Then she tells me to take a seat on the couch.

"Annabelle, what are your thoughts about your mum bringing you to see a therapist?"

I scan my brain for the right response. On more than a few occasions, I've heard Mom and Dad speak in whispered words:

Annabelle is so . . . shy.

Maybe all the moving is affecting her.

She just needs to make friends.

Dr. Varma tips her head as though I'm taking too long to answer.

"My thoughts are . . . that I don't need a therapist. No offense. Isn't this where people go when they're going crazy?"

"No, not exactly," Dr. Varma says. "Sometimes when there are big changes in a family, like your recent move to the United States, it can help you make a plan for your new life."

I'm not sure what she wants me to do with that, so I just sit there silently.

"Tell me about life at McManus!" Dr. Varma says that like it's the greatest thing ever.

I chew on my bottom lip.

"Consider this a place where you can empty out all of your feelings and nothing will ever leave this room. Now, go on, tell me about your new school. It can't be *that* bad," Dr. Varma says.

You don't know the half of it, lady, I think, and then I let it all fly. "I've been a student at

McManus Middle School for one week and so far I've"—I tick them off on my fingers as I speak—"forgotten my locker combination twice. Thrown out my nasty lunch three times. Gotten lost four times. And last, but not least, tossed my favorite pair of Converse in the trash."

Dr. Varma is writing nonstop, but pauses to gnaw on her pen eraser. "Why'd you throw away your shoes?"

"They're just not my style anymore," I say, looking down at my black leather Mary Janes. The real reason was that Rachael and everyone else was looking at my sneakers like they were from outer space.

"Interesting." Dr. Varma starts scribbling again.

"Why do you do that?"

"Do what?" Dr. Varma's eyes are intensely fixed on her notepad.

"Write all of this stuff down . . . like I'm some kind of experiment?"

She stops writing, looks up, and smiles. "Tell

me. In a perfect world, what would your life be like?"

"I don't know. I'd be back home in Germany, or even better, back in the UK. That's where my best friend, Mae, lives. And Mom would be retired already, so no more moving." Thinking about that makes my shoulders instantly relax.

"My job is to help you find a support system, to get you through this move and the time your mum will be gone," Dr. Varma says.

We sit there for a few moments silently. I gaze out the big windows next to the couch. Outside there are kids riding bikes, cars driving by, the whole Earth moving along. Meanwhile, my old life and my best friend are on another continent.

"Your mum tells me you're a techie and you make great videos. I would love to see your work one day," Dr. Varma says.

"I can show you now, if you'd like."

Dr. Varma claps her hands. "Absolutely!"

I grab my MacBook out of my knapsack,

open it up, click on the iMovie app, and show her a few clips on full-screen mode. The first one is a really old voiceover of me acting out an epic Lego battle. The other is a voiceover of me re-enacting the human-eating plant scene from my favorite movie, *Little Shop of Horrors*. Fake screams and all.

That one sends Dr. Varma into a fit of laughter.

"You have such a talent, Annabelle! It's interesting how you used the word experiment earlier. And while I certainly don't think *you* are an experiment, watching your videos made me think of one."

Now this lady's got my attention. "OK," I say, "what do you have in mind?"

"Clearly, your parents love you, and I can tell that you are a close-knit family. All those years braving new countries together, all you've ever had were each other. And just when you thought things were settling down, your mum and dad send you off into the wilderness! No wonder you told them you wanted to drop out of school!"

Yes! Finally, someone gets it!

"To be fair, they just want you to break out of your shyness and make new friends. And really, that's why I'm here, Annabelle. To help you come up with some strategies. But I think you just proved that it would be better if you're in control of this whole—for lack of a better word—*experiment*."

Control. Yes, I like that.

"So, how about you start a vlog?"

My eyes widen. "I'm listening," I say, loosening my crossed legs.

"You can use those movie-making skills and create a YouTube channel that features all of your vlogs."

I spring up off the couch, beyond excited. "THAT would be amazing!"

Dr. Varma jumps up with me and blurts: "You can try out some of the activities that they have at school and then vlog about them. Oh, you're going to be a natural in front of the camera, Annabelle!"

Whoa. Stop it right there.

"I'm sorry. What did you say?" I'm no longer jumping.

Dr. Varma still is, though. Her hair has released from its bun, falling in layers around her shoulders. "Did I say something wrong?" Dr. Varma snaps out of it.

I plop onto the leather couch. The cushions sigh right along with me. "It's just that I'm used to being *behind* the camera. Not in front of it."

"Why do you think that is?" she asks.

"I don't know. Maybe because, I would feel,"—I search for the right word—"*exposed.*"

"Ah, I see. But you know, it would be such a waste not to use this special skill to help you feel more comfortable in social situations. There has to be a way to compromise."

I scan my brain for how I could make that happen. Maybe it would work, but only if I could . . .

Ding! Ding! Ding! Dr. Varma's timer goes off.

"Saved by the bell!" I jump up off the couch. "Guess that means I'll be leaving."

"Not so fast, young lady. My next appointment isn't for another thirty minutes, and I saw that idea bubbling! I'm going to bring in your mum to discuss this further. We're on to something big here!"

Dr. Varma peeks her head into the waiting room. "May we see you for a moment, Sergeant Louis?"

Mom walks in and takes a seat next to me.

Dr. Varma tells her about how wonderful our intro session was, and then she looks at me. "Annabelle will tell you the rest."

I explain everything to Mom, and she looks really into the whole vlog idea. "But *if* I'm going to make a vlog," I say, "I have some conditions. First, the videos will be marked private. No one sees them except you guys, Dad, and Mae."

"Sounds easy," Dr. Varma cuts me off. "I'm no good with social media, but I'm sure you know what to do."

"Second, I'll use my middle name, Daphne, for the vlog."

Dr. Varma and Mom look at each other and nod.

"And third, even though the videos will be private, I refuse to be in front of the camera without some sort of disguise."

Mom laughs at that one. "Well, why would you want to go and do that?"

"I would die if I'm caught, Mom!"

"How dramatic!" Mom says. "OK, costumes, makeup, maybe even a wig. Oh, this will be fun!"

"Sounds like a fabulous plan, Annabelle," Dr. Varma says. "Now let's talk about what school activities you'll vlog about."

"Why can't I just vlog about stuff I see on television and in the news?" I ask.

"Let's take what you love—making movies—

and pair that with what we want to help you with, which is making friends at school."

"I saw on the school website that next week is Sports Day," Mom says.

The imaginary camera zooms in on me, and I explode into a pile of ashes. "I don't do sports," I blurt out. I had already cooked up the perfect excuse to be absent for Sports Day: food poisoning.

"Oh, but this is a fantastic way to start your vlog!" Dr. Varma says.

Mom gets all excited and says, "Ooh, and I have a great name for it—*Daphne Does It All*! Your first episode will be all about sports and how much *I know* you'll love them!"

I force a smile so hard, my cheeks hurt. Dr. Varma said I am in control. So I come up with the perfect name for my channel: *Daphne DOESN'T*. As in does nothing. Because I think everything about school and extracurricular activities is a waste of my time. None of this will bring Mae back, and there's not a sport in the world that'll keep me from missing Mom when she leaves. Instead of using the vlog to try new activities and make new friends at school, I'll prove how useless they all are in the first place. That'll show Mom and Dad that I was right all along: Homeschooling is a better choice for me.

While Mom and Dr. Varma sit there making plans, I'm drawing up my own for my first episode: "Daphne Definitely Doesn't Do Sports!"

8

HELLO, DAPHNE!

"Where are we going?" I ask as Mom hooks a left into the largest outdoor shopping center I've ever seen.

"I think you're going to love this place. It'll bring back some memories." Mom pulls into a parking space.

We walk to the stores. She stops in front of a store called Second Chance. In the display window, there's a mannequin wearing a vintage dress that looks straight out of the

Elizabethan era. Another mannequin looks like a detective with a long trench coat. And there's a rack full of jewelry from different parts of the world.

I am IN LOVE!

"Oh my goodness, Mom, this is like . . ." My skin gets all tingly just thinking about it.

"Trödelei!" Mom and I sing the word together.

Trödelei is this little thrift store in Berlin. Right outside of it is a stand that sells hot, fresh crepes filled with Nutella and topped with ice cream.

"Ready to get Daphne-fied?" Mom asks.

"Oh yeah!"

The movie in my head begins. *Cue music! Lights! Camera! Action!*

We swing open the door . . . annnnnd there isn't a soul here. Any second now, I'm expecting tumbleweeds to roll by.

Houselights down. Cameras off. Better yet, just unplug the whole set.

Second Chance is nearly double the size of

Trödelei. How can people just walk by all of this fabulous stuff? For cheap too! In Trödelei, you'd be lucky to have an aisle to yourself. Even still, that would only last a minute.

"Come in! Come in!" A woman with waist-long blond hair scurries over to us. She sounds so excited. I'm pretty sure we're her first customers of the day . . . and judging by how dark it's getting outside, we'll probably be her last.

"Welcome to my store. I'm the owner, Georgia."

"Thank you," Mom says. "I'm Wendy, and this is my daughter, Annabelle."

"Is there anything in particular you're looking for today?" Georgia asks.

"Well, Annabelle is working on . . ." Mom starts talking, and I kind of zone out looking at all the cool things in the store. A Harry Potter-style cloak. A collection of neon and glitter wigs. Feather boas. Old Hollywood wall art. I can see myself dressed as a Victorian duchess or even a British spy! All of this stuff is perfect for my vlog and for decorating my girl cave. Shut up and take ALL of my money!

Mom's rambling breaks me out of my zone. ". . . so she'll need to dress up in different outfits for her online show."

"What did you say?"

Mom is *forever* telling my business. First Dr. Varma. Now the thrift shop lady.

"I was telling Georgia all about your show."

"Online?" Sweet Georgia smiles so wide, her top dentures come undone. "You're gonna be on one of those new types of television? What do they call it, Halo?"

Hulu.

"Nothing on television, ma'am. This is a project . . . for school." I press my finger into Mom's back.

Mom gives me a look that says, *OK, I'll shut up.*

"Well, help yourselves, ladies," Georgia says. "We have plenty of goodies!"

Mom and I spend the next hour in Second Chance trying on everything and filling up two carts to bring Daphne and my girl cave to life.

When we get home, we order dinner and get right to work decorating the room where all of the Daphne magic will happen. Two hours later, the girl cave is complete, and it's everything I've ever dreamed of. A real place to call my own.

"Don't stay up too late, *Daphne*," Dad says before heading upstairs to his room.

"I won't, Dad."

Mom kisses my forehead and follows Dad up the basement stairs.

I sit in my girl cave, thinking about how awesome it is. There's film strip art on the walls; a little kitchenette full of soda pop, chips, and Twizzlers; a brand-new camera with a tripod; bright lights; my desk with two screens, my private YouTube channel all set up and ready to go. But even with all these cool things surrounding me, I feel incomplete.

My phone buzzes, and then I know exactly who's missing.

Mae: Good luck tomorrow . . . "Daphne."

9

SPORTS DAY

John walks into homeroom, all smiles. Right
away, I notice he's wearing cleats . . . with no
cleats (cleatless cleats?), basketball shorts, and
a football jersey. Annnnd for good measure, a
helmet's sticking out of his backpack. Not that I
should talk, with my no-name sneakers, baggy
sweats, and hot cocoa–stained T-shirt.

"I got a joke for you," John says, sitting down
next to me.

Here we go.

"Why did the football coach go to the bank?"

I'm sure John can see how thrilled I am, so he finishes the joke for me. "He wanted his quarter back!" John laughs so hard his entire body shakes.

"Good one," I say softly.

"Let me see your schedule," he says.

I pull it out of my notebook and hand him the paper of doom: lacrosse, football, and swimming.

"Nice! You picked the same sports I did."

"Not really. They stuck me wherever because I started school late."

Rachael arrives to homeroom fashionably late. Everything she's wearing is matchy-matchy princess perfect. And so begin the comments from her fans. . . .

Fan #1: "Are those the newest Adidas?"

Rachael: "Oh, these? They haven't hit the stores yet."

Fan #2: "Love the makeup today, girl!"

Rachael: "Oh, this? Just some waterproof mascara and cherry bomb ChapStick."

Every. Single. Boy. In class drools on the floor. Except John. The kid marches to the beat of his own drum.

The bell rings, and I make my way to the field out back.

"Wait up, Annabelle." John runs to catch up to me.

A whistle blows hard and loud from the field. "Hurry!" the teacher yells. "We have a lot to learn."

Twenty-one of us surround the teacher and his whiteboard full of drawings that look like hieroglyphics to me. *Xs*, *Os*, and lines are scribbled everywhere.

"Welcome to lacrosse! I'm Coach Carmine." He points to the teachers standing beside him. "This is your referee, Mr. Thomas, your umpire, Mrs. Locke, and your field judge, Mr. Williams. Now, who here has played lacrosse before?"

All the hands go up. But mine. Lovely.

And cue single focus zoom!

Of course everyone turns around and looks at me.

"So you're new to lacrosse, eh?" Coach Carmine smirks.

"She's new to this whole country!" someone calls out.

"I was born here but moved overseas when I was really young." I want to say all of that loud and proud enough to prove the point that I *am* American, but everything comes out in a whisper.

"Where did you move from?" Coach asks.

"Germany." My entire face is fixed on the grass.

"No lacrosse in Germany, I imagine," Coach says.

I shake my head. Not that I would know.

"We'll go easy on you, then," he says, trying to make me feel better.

Coach gives us a rundown of everything we need to know about the sport. The rules.

The equipment. The history. None of it sticks in my brain beyond the cool fact that lacrosse was invented by Native Americans, though Coach Carmine can't remember which nation.

Mrs. Locke passes out all the equipment to the players. She outfits me with full gear— helmet, shoulder guards, arm pads, gloves, and a netted stick—and positions me in front of the "goal crease" while the other teachers separate everyone into teams of ten. I start thinking up an escape plan. Maybe I could say I have to go to the bathroom and stay there until the game is over? But how would I get all of this equipment off by myself? And what would everyone think of me being in the bathroom for the entire game? Ugh!

"Relax. This will be fun." Mrs. Locke sees my panic through the helmet.

"All you have to do is try to stop the opposing team from scoring. That's it!"

Sure, lady. Sounds easy.

Mrs. Locke runs off and takes her spot as umpire.

Mr. Thomas screams, "PLAY!" He blows a whistle, and all chaos breaks loose.

The kids prance about with their nets in the air, running after this teeny-tiny ball as it dances around the field. If I didn't know any better, I'd think they were chasing butterflies. All that's missing are sunflowers, a rainbow in the sky, and Taylor Swift playing on repeat. It is the funniest thing I've seen in weeks. Laughter boils inside me, and all of a sudden I'm hunched over, completely unaware of the ball that's just landed smack into the goal.

The opposing team roars!

"Wake up, Annabelle!" one of the kids on my team calls out.

That wipes the smile right off my face.

John runs over to me. "Don't worry about him. Just try your best to block the ball from going in."

Easy for him to say.

Ladies and gentlemen, I present the pleasant sounds of the next three quarters:

Smack!

Ouch!

Whoops!

Oof!

Coach Carmine blows the whistle. Game over. The score is . . . 8 to 0. I hear the shouts immediately:

"Nice job, Annabelle!"

"Yeah, thanks for nothing!"

I can't get out of this stupid lacrosse *costume* fast enough.

I hate lacrosse. I hate this school. I hate moving. I hate TDY. I zip across the field, tears flying in the wind, but you-know-who is already following me inside.

"Wait up!" John has a friend with him. "Where are you going?" he asks.

"To the bathroom . . . for the rest of the day," I mutter.

We stand in the empty cafeteria, silent for a few seconds, until girl-with-the-friendly-smile speaks. "Don't be silly! You can't hang out in there. Teachers will mark you as cut, and then you'll have bigger problems than lacrosse."

I stare at my shoes, wondering if it'd be worth it.

"I'm Clairna Joseph, by the way."

I notice her eyes are friendly too. A deep, warm brown, just like Mom's.

"Nice to meet you, but I'm not doing any of the other sports. This is just—"

"Not your thing?" Clairna tilts her head. "I hate Sports Day too. Most of *our kind* do."

"What's that supposed to mean—our kind?" I ask.

"Oh, come on," John begins. "All schools have their cliques. There's the popular clique."

"And the jock clique!" Clairna chimes in.

"Oh yeah, and the artsy clique," I add, remembering the kids at the lunch table who were building chicken nugget sculptures the other day.

We all laugh.

"And then there's . . . us." Clairna gets all

serious. "The not-so-athletic, totally unpopular, unfashionable clique."

"Speak for yourself, Clairna. I always rock the latest gear." John points to his cleatless cleats, and we start laughing all over again.

"Don't beat yourself up. For what it's worth, our whole team sucked," Clairna says.

"Football is next. Come on, you're not gonna miss that, are you?" John does a macho man pose.

"I promise it will be fun . . . and funny." Clairna chuckles.

I chew on my inner cheek. Maybe she's right. At least I *do* know what football is—even though they say it funny here in the States. Dad and I pronounce it *fútbol*. Every four years, Dad watches the World Cup and cheers for Brazil. Five wins is nothing to sneeze at.

"OK, I'll do it."

"Cool!" Clairna does a little happy dance. By the time we reach the front of McManus, we've already missed the bus to Tiger Stadium.

Mr. Fingerlin is directing students to other activities.

"Very late, I see." Mr. Fingerlin gives us the *tsk-tsk* voice.

"We had to stop at the bathroom," John says.

"You guys can catch this one." Mr. Fingerlin taps the door of bus number 634.

We climb on, and a few streetlights and turns later, the bus pulls up and we run onto the sidelines. A game is already in progress. According to the scoreboard, the score is 7–6, and they are in the final stretch.

What a relief! Now we won't have to play. The teacher will just mark our names on the attendance list. And now I can get this God-awful part of the day over with.

"Lopez, Joseph, new kid—you're late!" the coach yells as we run to the bench.

"Coach Tillman, this is Annabelle Louis." John uses my full name like it matters.

"Quick! Joseph, Lopez, play defense." Coach

Tillman sounds like Darth Vader from *Star Wars*.

Clairna and John run to the field, slapping their helmets on.

"Louis, I'm gonna have you substitute kick for a field goal," he explains. "Twenty yards. Get 'em."

He hands me a helmet, taps me on the shoulder, and my whole body goes flying toward the field. Field goal? Kick the ball? Everyone is staring at me, and I'm having flashbacks to the first day all over again.

There's a triangular device holding the ball. It doesn't look anything like what I've seen in the World Cup. Four years is a long time. Maybe they changed the style of the ball?

I throw John a look, and he mutters through his helmet, "Just kick and we run it to the end, I guess?"

Coach Tillman blows his whistle.

I take a deep breath, my eyes on the brown,

pointy-looking ball. I swing my right foot back, and BAM! The ball goes soaring, kids are screaming, "Whoa!" And I! Feel! Amazing!

As soon as the ball hits the ground, I gain speed right behind it and start kicking and running at the same time. The ball isn't moving like it does in the World Cup. It's wobbling, really.

Kids are gaining on me, and I can hear them screaming:

"What is she doing?"

"This is hilarious!"

"This ain't soccer!"

Finally the ball passes the white line. That means I scored for my team, right? Take that, haters! I jump and spin around, my fists pumping to the sky. Several students are laughing and rolling on the ground. And suddenly my stomach begins eating itself. Clairna and John run over to me.

"I think you were playing a different sport, Annabelle," Clairna says.

"But he said drive it to the line, or something like that . . . right?"

And cue sweat beads!

The kids are still rolling, and Coach Tillman is running our way. "That was something else, kid," he says. Then he yells at everyone on the ground. "Get up, show's over. Get to lunch!"

Apparently, I was playing *fútbol* . . . as in soccer. Not as in *American* football.

There's no way I'm getting on that bus where every single teammate is waiting to finish making fun of me. Coach Tillman agrees to let Clairna, John, and me wait for a later bus.

* * *

By the time we get back to McManus, there are fifteen minutes left to eat lunch. While Clairna and John head to the cafeteria, I tell them that I brought lunch from home and I have to grab it from my locker.

Which is a lie.

I find an empty janitor's closet. It's not my

girl cave, and even though I'm surrounded by buckets of dirty mop water and a couple of rat traps, it'll do. I pull out a granola bar from my knapsack and text Mae.

Me: That's it. I quit. I mean it this time.

Mae: Hey, *amiga*! What happened?

Me: Sports happened.

Mae: :(

Me: I'm not going to the last class. Faking sick and going to the nurse. Excuse? Food poisoning. Easy to believe when today's lunch is dog food dressed up as something called a sloppy joe.

Mae: Good excuse! Bad lunch! What's your last sport?

Me: Swimming. And don't you even think about it!

Mae: But you swim so fast! Remember all the times you beat me on holiday in the Dominican Republic?

Just then, there's a loud bang on the door.

Me: Gotta go. Janitor alert.

Mae: <3

"Annabelle, we know you're in there." It's Clairna. "You're not the first seventh grader to hide in here on a bad day."

I undo the lock and open the door. John and Clairna walk in, followed by another kid.

And he doesn't look too happy. "It stinks in here," he says. "Why would you hide in the janitor's closet when there's the paper supply closet two doors down?"

John takes a deep breath. "I love the smell of paper."

Clairna claps. "Focus, people. Annabelle, Navdeep. Navdeep, Annabelle."

"Just call me Nav."

"Um, hi, Nav," I say softly.

Clairna gives Nav a rundown of how awfully embarrassing lacrosse and football were.

Thanks for telling all of my business, Clairna!

But Nav doesn't laugh one bit. In fact, he looks like he . . . understands.

"My family moved here from India when I was in fifth grade. They just plopped me in school with a bunch of kids who made fun of my English and the way I dressed and the lunch I'd bring from home. And sports? Forget it! I knew nothing about American football or lacrosse."

It makes me feel better. Sort of. But it won't make this day end any sooner.

"I can't go to swim class," I announce.

"This is happening." Clairna marches me out of the janitor's closet.

The four of us walk past the main office and straight out the front doors. The Linden YMCA bus is waiting to take a group of us to the last activity of the day.

Mr. Fingerlin is waiting outside. "Swim

classes will be held separately for boys and girls!" he announces.

Out of the blue, I feel someone staring at me. It's Rachael. She looks at me for a microsecond and then turns around.

The bus doors open. Rachael goes on first and her adoring fans follow.

Clairna and I grab a seat in the back of the bus. For the next ten minutes, we're stuck listening to Rachael and friends.

The bus pulls up to the Linden YMCA, and we're led straight to the locker room to change into our swimsuits. That's when I realize I've made the biggest mistake of my life: letting Mom pack my bag.

Strike #1: She forgot my swim cap. My hair will hate me for this.

Strike #2: The swimsuit she's picked has ducks on it . . . DUCKS!!!! And I haven't worn it in, I don't know, YEARS!!!!

Meanwhile, Rachael looks like a supermodel in her red, white, and blue striped tankini.

A loud whistle sounds from outside. "File in line, ladies, and let's get to work!"

As we get in line, one of Rachael's friends—the one with a fake smile and an extra side of drool, special just for Rachael—says, "Love the ducks, Annabelle. Slay, girl, *slay*!"

And cue laughter!

Clairna pinches me as a reminder: *Block it out, girl.*

Coach Hewitt reviews three techniques with us: breaststroke, forward stroke, and backstroke. Surprisingly, I know how to do them all.

"And now, for a little bit of friendly competition, let's have a race for the butterfly stroke!" Coach Hewitt announces.

She splits us up, and surprise, surprise! Rachael is my partner.

Clairna is two girls ahead of me. Coach Hewitt blows her whistle. Clairna jumps in the water and starts swimming for her life. But by the time Clairna reaches one end, her competitor is already circling back.

The line moves up swiftly, and it's finally my turn. Coach begins the countdown. Rachael and I bend our knees in three, two, one . . . blast off!

My legs don't stop for one second. I push faster, harder. My hand touches the pool wall. I do a flip under the water, press my feet against the wall and swim to the other side, my hair flailing all around me. When I touch the starting wall and lift my head above the water, Coach is blowing the whistle and Clairna is screaming, "Oh my God, you won!"

I did? I want to shout. I want to jump. I want to pump my fist to the sky. This day didn't turn out so bad after all!

Rachael shakes my hand and says, "Congratulations."

We get out of the pool, and before I can reach my towel, it happens. I knew it was coming. My hair becomes a leafy bush. My swimsuit is so small that the ducks on my butt have disappeared and become the biggest wedgie known to man!

"Might be time for a new swimsuit," Coach Hewitt whispers softly, so no one hears.

But a couple of girls are already laughing at me, and I'm not sure if it's because of the massive wedgie or the fact that my hair is slowly turning into an oak tree.

10

VLOG

As soon as I get home, I take a shower, change, and head straight to my girl cave in the basement. I'm itching to do my first vlog, and I know exactly what I'm going to say.

First, I have to transform myself into Daphne.

I find a silver sequin shirt with bell-shaped sleeves and a neon green feather boa. I add the hot pink framed glasses, and the finishing touch is the wig—straight, long, and orange. My whole outfit is so ugly, it's perfect!

Mom even got me some makeup so I can go the extra mile and *put my face on*. So I apply a light pink lip gloss and rose-tinted blush. If only Rachael could see me now!

When I look in the mirror, I don't even recognize myself.

Hello, Daphne! Let's do this!

I set up the tripod in front of my chair, flash on the lights, and click the record button on the video camera.

At first I sit there and don't say anything. My stomach feels funny. I can't do this. Why am I chickening out of this thing?

I whip out my cell phone and let my fingers fly.

Me: That's it, I quit! I don't do sports and apparently I can't even make this vlog.

For the next ten minutes, I pace the room contemplating the meaning of life and waiting for Mae to respond.

Mae: Sorry, was watching the telly. No

excuses, Annabelle. Just be yourself. Make the video. It's not like anyone is watching it . . . well, except ME! I can't wait. Now, go on!

Ugh! She's right. This is just an experiment. What's the worst that could happen?

I start over and hit the record button. My shoulders loosen up, I think back on every terrible part of Sports Day and why everything about sports is plain awful. Like magic, the words start coming out. And I'm not sure why, but I'm speaking in a British accent.

"Hey, what's up, guys? It's Daphne, and welcome to my social experiment. Today's vlog is entitled 'Daphne *Definitely* Doesn't Do Sports!'

"I'll be talking to you about the top five things I hate about sports:

"Number one: Too many rules. Throw the ball, catch it, kick it. Touch the pool wall with one hand. Don't hold the ball longer than four seconds in the goal crease. How about . . . no?

"Number two: Spaghetti arms. If you are like

me—shapeless, made of parallel lines and noodle arms—sports will never, ever be a good thing!

"Number three: Getting it wrong in front of everyone and having them laugh at you.

"Number four: It's dirty outside. Why would anyone want to play where there's mud and bugs?

"Number five: Last but not least . . . everything. No, seriously. The sweat. The growling. The falling. The water up your nose. The wedgies. It's all awful!

"So there you have it! The top five things I hate about sports and why I will NEVER do them again. My mum wanted me to give sports a real effort because, according to her, 'you can make friends.' And I did make a couple today. Sort of. But still, this sports thing is not for me. Thank you for watching this video! Leave a comment if you wish! Or not."

When I'm done recording, I import the video to iMovie and start editing. I add in a few animation effects. Mud flying. Spaghetti splatting against the screen and sliding down to a slow death.

By the time I'm done with everything, I'm itching to show everyone. But Dad is asleep, Mom's at Fort Dix, and it's three in the morning in the UK.

I decide to leave the video public for a bit so Mae can see it. I send her a text.

Me: Just uploaded my first vlog. It's public, so hurry up and watch. Eeep!

I wait a few minutes, hoping that she's up reading and will text me back. But she doesn't.

UGH!

11

BUSTED!

We're not allowed to have cell phones in class, but the next day I break the rules because Mae still hasn't texted me back and I'm dying to know what she thinks of my vlog.

Third period, I have computer class. The class size is pretty large, and when the teacher isn't looking, I check my phone.

Mae: Just watched your video, and HOLY MOLY 46 views? I thought you were keeping it private?

Forty-six views? Every organ in my digestive system seems to squeeze into one giant mass.

Mrs. Gironda starts her lesson on Microsoft Excel, but I don't have time to listen to this. I need to log into my YouTube account ASAP and change the privacy setting. We're not allowed to go on any social media during class, so I have to do it from my phone . . . which I'm not supposed to have. I click on the link, go to my channel, and see that I no longer have 46 views. I have 98!!!!! And there are comments:

CousinHilary1996: This is hilarious!

ItsACaliThing: Omg I hate sports too!

BossGirl13: When will you post your next vlog?

I need a towel to wipe the sweat off my hands . . . and EVERY SINGLE PART OF ME!

I smell Mrs. Gironda before she even speaks. Mentholated cough drops with a dash of vanilla-scented perfume.

"Annabelle Louis? Please tell me you're not playing on your phone in class."

"I'm sorry. I was just putting it away."

"Rules are rules, young lady. Hand it over."

The whole class is staring at me now. John shakes his head as if to say, "Just give in."

I hand my phone to Mrs. Gironda.

"You can have it back at the end of the day."

I decide that I will just go to my locker to grab my MacBook during lunch. The bell rings, and I hurry to my locker. That's when I realize I LEFT MY MACBOOK AT HOME! And I can't even log into my account on someone else's phone because I don't remember the password. Because it's saved on my phone! And my laptop!

It's official. MY LIFE IS RUINED!

At lunch, Navdeep, Clairna, John, and I go outside for some fresh air. Clairna's phone beeps with a notification. She checks it and starts giggling.

"What's so funny?" John asks.

"YouTube always sends alerts of new videos that they recommend for me. I've never heard of this channel, but check it out."

I'm standing next to John when she hands him the phone.

And drumroll, please . . .

I see myself pop up on the screen, and I ALMOST DIE!

John is cracking up. He doesn't even flinch when he sees my face and then Daphne's.

In fact, none of them do. They don't recognize that it's me . . . At. All. But still, my insides flip-flop around and I feel my face get hot. I have to hurry up and get my phone back before this goes any further.

Later on, when the dismissal bell rings, I zip to Mrs. Gironda's room. The door is locked, and there's a sign on it:

SICK—WENT HOME EARLY!

This has to be a cruel joke. Kids are walking down the hall. I see them on their phones, hear *my* British accent coming from *their* speakers.

"This Daphne chick needs to make another video." A kid passes by and looks at me as he says this.

Both of my hands rise to cover my face. HOW DID THIS HAPPEN? Five billion videos on YouTube and they find *mine*?

When I get home, I race down to the basement, swing open the door to my girl cave, and open my MacBook. Right away, I get a FaceTime from Mae.

"Oh my goodness, go to your channel right now." Her voice is all business.

When I get to YouTube, I can't believe my eyes.

I'm screaming, then Mae starts screaming, then we're both laughing and screaming at the same time. Soon Mom is flying down the stairs to ask what's wrong with me. But when she sees me and Mae looking happy, she starts screaming too.

"What are we screaming about?" Mom starts laughing.

I show her my video, which she still hasn't seen.

The guys from DudePerfect shared my video with the comment, "THIS IS PERFECT!"

And now it has gone from 98 views to 453 views in not even a couple of hours! It's been shared 17 times, and I have 28 subscribers.

"Hi, Mrs. Louis." Mae waves from the computer. "Do you see our popular girl, Daphne?"

"Mae, I love it!" Mom says. "I'm going to call Dr. Varma right now and share the good news."

Mom calls her on speakerphone. "Dr. Varma," she says when the doctor picks up. "Annabelle, Mae, and I here. Have you heard the news?"

"Yes, I see Annabelle's video is doing very well!" Dr. Varma says. "Annabelle, I thought you were going to keep it private?"

Mae chimes in, "I say you keep this going. Just look at the views now!"

I'm up to 506 views, 21 shares, and 30 subscribers.

I tell everyone I have to sleep on all of this. My fingers itch to do what I do best—make myself invisible and click private. But something inside me says, "Keep going."

12

BREAKING THE RULES

"I see you took matters into your own hands and didn't name the vlog *Daphne Does It All*. You're a take-charge kind of girl," Dr. Varma says.

"Thank you . . . I think?"

"And you have yet to make it private?" she asks.

"I'm up to 1,203 views, and that's just for the sports video. I posted a quick school lunch video right before I came here, and it's already gotten 736 views. Every time I tell myself to click private, something stops me."

"And tell me, is anything different at school? Is it still this awful place that you want to drop out of?"

"Well, not exactly. I met a few people. Like Rachael. She's really popular, but she barely knows I exist. And then there's John—he's funny. And Clairna and Navdeep are pretty cool too. I eat lunch with them."

"It sounds like you're finding your way at McManus."

I guess I am.

"I was thinking about something. The videos are great, but I'm not convinced you fully accomplished the goal," Dr. Varma says.

"What do you mean?"

"I was thinking that we should find something you *do* like to do," Dr. Varma says. "Any ideas on what the next topic could be?"

She's already pulling up the McManus webpage on her tablet.

I can tell where this is going.

"I think I found the perfect activity for you, Annabelle!"

Note to self: must find a way to hack McManus's website and prevent doctor access.

Dr. Varma moves to my couch so we can see it together.

And there it is:

Audition for the Drama Department's Fall Play:

Little Shop of Horrors!

Monday, October 1 at 3:30 p.m.

No need to have anything prepared. Come as you are!

Dr. Varma flips one arm to her side and does spirit fingers. "Didn't you say this was your favorite movie? Oh this will be *perfect*! I can see it now: 'Daphne Does Drama.'"

How about . . . Daphne definitely does NOT?

TALK ABOUT IT!

1. Annabelle moves around a lot, but moving to new schools is still difficult for her. What are some ways you could help a new student at your school?

2. Phones and social media help people connect even over great distances. Annabelle keeps in touch with her best friend Mae over the phone. Do you have any friends who live far away that you keep in touch with over the phone? How does keeping in touch with Mae help Annabelle at her new school?

3. Annabelle tells Dr. Varma that something inside her tells her not to make her videos private. What do you think that is? What are some ways making her vlogs public can help her at her new school?

WRITE IT DOWN!

1. Annabelle uses her filmmaking hobby to help her deal with changes at her new home and school. Brainstorm some ideas and make a list of hobbies you could use to journal your life.

2. Annabelle is considered an outsider by some of her classmates. Write about a time you've felt like an outsider at school.

3. Annabelle decorates her girl cave with things she found at Second Chance. Write down what you would decorate your room with if you were making vlogs like Annabelle.

ABOUT THE AUTHOR

Tami Charles writes picture books, middle grade and young adult fiction, and nonfiction. Her middle grade novel debut, *Like Vanessa*, is a Junior Library Guild selection. *Like Vanessa* was also selected by the American Bookseller's Association for the Indies Introduce Kids List. Tami is the author of four more books forthcoming with Albert Whitman & Co., Candlewick, and Charlesbridge. She resides in New Jersey with her husband and son.